D0246434

Grave Dirt

by

E. E. Richardson

First published in 2008 in Great Britain by
Barrington Stoke Ltd
18 Walker Street, Edinburgh, EH3 7LP

www.barringtonstoke.co.uk

ISBN: 978-1-84299-521-1

Printed in Great Britain by Bell & Bain Ltd

A Note from the Author

This story grew from the idea of the grave doll. I think dolls are creepy. No matter how life-like they are, they still don't look really alive.

That got me thinking about life and death. We don't have the power to make things come to life. We can't bring people back from the dead. But what if we could? It might not be a good thing. People might not come back the same as when they left. And what if you did it wrong? You might bring back the wrong person. You might bring back someone who was better off left dead ...

Contents

Chapter 1
Luke

It had been a bad day from the start.

It was a Thursday. Darren didn't get on with Thursdays. He had all his worst lessons. French, PE, two hours of Science, and then Maths.

Even PE was no fun. At this time of year they had tennis. Darren was rubbish at tennis.

Luke was good at it. He was good at every sport. He was top in all his classes, too. He never seemed to see how hard it was for Darren.

"We should bunk off," Luke said after PE. "You can come over to my house. I'll show you that new game I just got. It's really cool."

"We can't," Darren told him. "We've got Science next. We still need to finish the work from last week. I can't write it up until we've got the results."

"Just make some up!" Luke gave a shrug. "Who's going to notice?"

Darren let out a sigh. "Oh, Luke, come on," he said. "I need to get good marks this time. I got a D for my last project."

"Who cares? It's just Science." Luke did his trainers up and stood up. "I'm going home. You should come with me."

But Darren shook his head. "We need to get this done."

"Well, you go to Science, then," Luke said. He grabbed his bag. "You can get the results, and I'll copy them off you. I'll see you after school." He left the changing rooms.

Darren ran after him. "Luke, come on! Don't leave me here on my own. You're meant to be working on this with me."

Luke just waved at him. "See you later, loser," he shouted back. He laughed and ran over to the fence. Darren watched him jump over it and run off.

He knew right then that it would be a crappy day.

He had no idea how bad it would get.

****

Darren was in a bad mood for all of Science. He knew he was going to get the work wrong. Why hadn't he just gone home with Luke?

Luke was his best friend, but he drove Darren nuts some days. Luke never had to worry. Things were easy for him. He could do what he felt like and still be the best in the class. Darren had to work hard to do even half as well.

Luke got to sit at home and play games while Darren was stuck in class. And he'd still end up with better marks than Darren. It was so unfair.

He didn't go over to Luke's house at lunch. He was still a bit annoyed, and he knew Luke'd just laugh at him. He wouldn't get why Darren even cared. So Darren stayed at school and went to Maths.

He soon wished he hadn't. It was boring as hell. He was half asleep by the end of school. He walked home in a bit of a daze.

On the way, he saw there'd been an accident. There was a massive dent in the railings on Bank Street. It looked like a car had crashed into them. He could see broken glass on the road.

4

A mobile phone lay in the gutter on the other side of the road. It had been smashed to bits.

Seeing the mobile all smashed up made Darren feel a bit sick. The car must have hit someone. And it had to have hit them hard. The phone had been thrown a long way. Darren tried not to think about it.

When he got home, he saw his mum's car on the drive. That was odd. She hadn't said she'd be home early. He let himself in with his key.

His mum was in the living room. As Darren came in, she stood up. Her face was pale and her eyes were red. It was easy to see she'd been crying.

And that was when he knew.

He could see the broken phone in his mind. It had been so smashed up it had been hard to tell what it was. It could have been a music player. It could have been a Gameboy. But he'd known right away it was a phone.

He'd known because Luke had one just like it.

"Darren –" his mum started to say. Darren didn't wait for her to say more. He just turned and ran away from her up the stairs.

He didn't want to hear her say the words. He already knew what they would be.

He already knew that Luke was dead.

Chapter 2
The Key

"Darren? We have to go soon," his dad said from the doorway. His voice was soft.

Most days Darren's dad just yelled up the stairs. But no one yelled at Darren at the moment. It was as if they thought the noise would make him shatter.

They might be right.

"In a minute, Dad," Darren said. His own voice sounded flat to him. It was too hard to try and put life in it. He didn't feel like he had any life to spare.

"What are you looking for?" His dad came into the room. He was dressed all in black. So was Darren. They were on their way to Luke's funeral.

But Darren wasn't quite ready. "I can't find my black socks," he said. He knew he had a pair. They should be in his top drawer. Why couldn't he find them?

"Just wear your grey ones," his dad said, with a kind smile. "No one's going to see them."

"No! I need my black ones!"

Luke was dead. He was being *buried*. The least Darren could do was wear the right socks.

His dad was silent for a moment. "I'll see if I can find you a pair of mine," he said, and left.

Darren's parents just did what he said now. Even if he screamed and shouted. It was creepy. It was like all the rules had died with

Luke. The rest of the world had just stopped making sense.

It made him feel like he was floating in space. Like he had nothing left to hold on to.

And he still couldn't find his stupid socks!

Darren yanked the drawer all the way out. As he did, he heard something fall down the back. He pulled the other drawers out to look.

It was a key. A dirty old iron key. He picked it up and stared at it.

It was the key to Mad Mary's house. Darren felt like his heart had stopped.

It was years since he'd thought of Mad Mary. She was the old woman who'd lived next door. She'd died when he was a kid.

He hadn't been too sad about it. She must have been over a hundred. And he hadn't liked her much. She'd given him the creeps.

Mad Mary had said she could do magic. She'd kept telling everyone that she could curse people. Anyone she didn't like was going to get a curse on them.

That had been most people. She hadn't been a very nice old lady.

She'd given Darren the key a few days before she died.

"I will be dead soon," she had told him. "When I am, you must do a spell for me. In my house, there is a box hidden under the floor. It contains a grave doll. You must fill the doll up with dirt from my grave and a drop of blood. Dirt is death and blood is life. It's an old, old magic that will let my ghost come back. Do it or I'll put a curse on you."

He hadn't done it, of course. He knew that Mad Mary was nuts. None of her spells were real. And why would he want her ghost to come back anyway? He hadn't even liked her.

But Darren had kept the key. It didn't seem right to just throw it away. Someone might find it and use it to get into her house. So he'd left it in the back of a drawer and forgotten about it.

And now here it was.

Darren stared at the key. He kept thinking about what Mad Mary had said. *It's an old, old magic that will let my ghost come back.*

It was total crap. He knew that. He did know that.

But … what if it wasn't? What if there was a tiny, tiny chance that it was real?

What if there was a way to bring Luke back?

"Darren?" His dad had come back into the room. Darren jumped and hid the key in his pocket.

"Oh! Er, yeah?" he said. His voice shook a bit. He was sure that he looked guilty. His dad would take one look at him and know what he'd been thinking.

But his dad just held out a pair of black socks. "You can wear these. Now, come on," he said. "It's time to go."

****

The funeral was hard for Darren. A lot of people cried, but he didn't. He couldn't stop thinking about the key.

The priest kept saying that Luke was in heaven. That he was with his gran and his dead uncle. Like that was meant to be a good thing. Like it should make them feel better.

There might not even *be* a heaven. And if there was, Luke shouldn't be there. He should be here, with his friends. He didn't belong up in heaven.

Darren closed his hand around the key.

It would be crazy to try and call Luke's ghost up. It would be crazy ... and wrong.

But this was wrong too. Luke being dead was just wrong. And maybe now Darren had a chance to set it right.

How could he not take it?

Chapter 3
Mad Mary's House

No one lived in Mad Mary's house now. It had been up for sale for ages.

A few different people had moved in over the years. And then moved out. None of them had stayed for very long. They'd all said that the house had a bad feel to it. People didn't like being in it.

That was good news for Darren. It made it much easier to sneak in and hunt for the doll.

"I'm going to go for a walk," he told his mum that night.

"All right." She was happy to let him.
Perhaps she thought it was a good sign. He'd
spent most of the time since Luke died shut up
in his room.

His mum wouldn't be so happy if she knew
what he was up to.

Darren had waited for it to get dark. The
key he had was for the back door of Mad
Mary's house. He didn't want to be seen going
round there.

The empty house was in a bad state. The
back garden looked like a jungle. No one had
cut the plants down for years. He had to fight
past brambles to get to the back door.

He hardly needed to have a key. The wood
was so rotten he could have just smashed it.
It felt slimy under his hand.

He got the key out anyway. It fitted the
lock, but the door was stiff. Darren had to kick
it to get it open.

Inside the house there was a bad smell of rot. The floor was thick with dust, and so was the air. When Darren had opened the door he'd sent up a big cloud of it. The dust made him cough and made his skin itch.

He saw that he was in the kitchen. The old cupboards and things were still here. They'd been white once, but now they were yellow. They were all covered in spider's webs.

There was a light switch on the wall. Darren pressed it, but it didn't work.

He wished he had a torch. It was too late to go back for one now.

What was he doing here? This was crazy. He had no real idea what he was looking for. A grave doll. What did that look like?

He didn't even know if it was still here. Or if it existed at all. Maybe Mad Mary had made it all up. She was mad, after all.

16

But he had to look. The picture of Luke's coffin was stuck in his head. He saw it when he closed his eyes.

Luke shouldn't be dead. It wasn't fair. It wasn't right. And if the grave doll could bring him back, then Darren had to have it.

He tried to think what Mad Mary had told him. She'd said that it was in a box hidden under the floor. But where under the floor? Which room? It was such a long time since she'd died ...

It couldn't be in this room. The kitchen floor had old stone tiles all over it. The box had to be in one of the rooms with wooden floor-boards.

He went deeper into the house.

The next room must have been the dining room. There was nothing in it now. That was a good thing, as it was too dark to see. In the kitchen, he'd had a bit of light from the door. In here there was none at all.

Darren took a step forward. The boards under his feet creaked and wobbled.

How could he tell if one of them was loose? They all felt loose! He kept one hand on the wall to keep his balance.

How was he going to find anything in a pitch black house?

He had to stop and think. Where would Mad Mary hide her treasure? In the living room? Under the stairs? Up in her bedroom?

That seemed like the best place to start. Her bedroom must be one of the rooms upstairs. There was no way to guess which one. He'd have to search them all.

Darren made his way out into the hall. The only way to find it was to go along the wall. It was just as dark as the last room.

It was hard to work out where he was. Where were the stairs? They should be more or less in front of him. He let go of the wall and took slow, careful paces. He didn't want to trip when he hit the bottom step.

The stairs shouldn't be that far off. Maybe just a few steps? He counted them out. One, two –

Crack!

On the third step, his foot went through the floor.

Chapter 4
The Doll

Darren yelled out in shock as he fell. He was sure he was going to break his neck. He would smash through the floor and bleed to death. No one would ever find his body. They wouldn't know to look for him in here.

But only his leg went down the hole. He swore. That was a near miss. That could have been bad.

His leg had gone in up to the knee. He'd scraped it, but it didn't seem too bad. He didn't think he'd done anything worse to it.

He pulled his foot out slowly. As he did, he felt his shoe hit something. He stuck his hand down the hole to grope around.

It was gross under the floor. The dust was as thick as cotton wool. He tried not to think about what his hand was touching.

Darren found the edge of a box. He dragged it towards him and pulled it up out of the hole. He had to break the floor-boards a bit more to get the box out.

It was about the size of a tissue box. He couldn't tell what was in it. He didn't want to poke around in it here in the dark. He wanted to wait until he could see it properly. Maybe it was full of rat poison – or worse.

Darren made his way back out of the house. He stuck close to the wall all the way. He didn't want to fall through the floor again. He might be hurt a lot worse the next time.

He couldn't see much better out in the garden. And he didn't want to stand under a street light. He locked the door and went back to his house.

"Darren?" his mum called out as he went in.

"Yeah, it's me." He ran up the stairs before she could come out and see the box.

When he got up to his room he turned the light on. The box was full of some kind of cloth. He lifted it up to see what was under it.

It was a human skull. But it was too small to belong to an adult. He was holding a dead baby!

Darren nearly dropped the box. But then he got a better look at it.

It wasn't a real skull. It looked like it was made of bone, but the teeth were all wrong. They were far too sharp. And the eye sockets didn't look right. They were too narrow and pointy.

Not a dead baby. Just a creepy doll.

The grave doll.

It was real.

Darren took the doll out of the box. The skull face was hard and bony but the doll's body was soft. It felt lumpy. He wasn't sure he wanted to know what the body was stuffed with.

The top of the skull was on a hinge. You could open it up to put things inside.

Things like a handful of grave dirt.

Darren took a slow, deep breath. Now that he had the doll in his hands ...

It looked nasty. It looked scary. It looked real.

What if Mad Mary had told him the truth? What if this doll really *could* bring Luke's ghost back?

A wild hope rose up inside him. He could see Luke again. They could talk. Darren could say he was sorry for not bunking off that day. He could say good-bye.

That was what he wanted most. A chance to say good-bye. And now he was holding that chance in his hands.

He had to get back to the graveyard.

****

Darren left the house in a hurry. He didn't stop to talk to his mum and dad. They'd think it was odd for him to go out again so soon. But he couldn't wait for even one more day. He had to see Luke again. He put the doll into his schoolbag and set off.

It took half an hour to walk to the graveyard. When he got there, the front gates were locked. It didn't really matter. The walls were high, but very old. There were lots of cracks and loose bricks to help him climb.

When he dropped down on the other side, it was pitch black. There was no moon, and no light in the graveyard. The lights on the road were blocked by the trees.

This time Darren *did* have a torch with him. The problem was that he didn't want to use it. What if someone saw the light? How could he explain what he was doing? He knew how crazy it would sound.

He knew it was crazy, but he didn't care. He had to do it.

It was cold among the graves. Really cold. It was as if the stones sucked all the heat out. Once he tripped and put his hand on one. It was like touching a block of ice.

It was creepy as hell.

Darren turned the torch on for a second. He could see a hill up ahead. He thought that Luke's grave was up there. It was hard to be sure. It all looked so different in the dark.

The sound of his feet in the grass was all he could hear. Even so, he felt like someone was watching him. He kept turning round to check there was no one there.

Darren made it to the top of the hill. He could smell fresh dirt and flowers. He turned the torch back on.

It lit up a fresh grave. Luke's grave.

This was it.

Chapter 5
Grave Robber

Darren stood in front of the grave. It was hard to think that Luke could be under there. He knew it, but he didn't really believe it. It didn't feel real.

That wasn't Luke under the ground. It was just a body. Dead skin and bone. The real Luke had to be somewhere else.

And surely if Darren called, he would come back.

Darren took a slow, deep breath. He lifted the doll out of his bag.

It felt too heavy for what it was. As if it was more than just a doll. As if the magic in it made it heavy. The hairs on the back of his neck stood up.

But the magic wouldn't work yet. He had to finish the spell.

Darren's hands shook as he took the spade out of his bag. It was a little plastic one like you used on the beach. It felt sick and twisted to be using it here.

He knew in his head that the coffin was a long way down. He could dig all night and still not get near it. All he was going to do was scrape a bit of dirt from the top. Just one quick scoop of the spade.

It was still the hardest thing he'd ever done.

"Sorry, Luke," he whispered to the grave. "But I have to. The spell won't work without it."

He dug the spade into the ground.

It felt like an alarm would go off. A spotlight would come down from the sky. Someone would catch him digging and it would be in all the papers. *Boy Digs up Best Friend's Grave to Do Black Magic.*

But there was no alarm. Darren lifted up the top of the doll's head. He poured the scoop of dirt into the skull.

In the dark, it was like he was looking at the doll's brains. He felt sick.

Darren set the doll down on the ground. He felt hot and itchy, as if he was ill. He took a pin out of his pocket.

Just one drop of blood. That was all it needed. Just one drop of blood, and then he'd see Luke again.

He jabbed the pin into his thumb. As the blood welled up, he shook his hand over the skull. Just to be extra sure, he wiped his thumb on the side of it. Some of his blood had to have got into the dirt.

Blood and dirt. The spell was done. Darren stood back.

"Luke?" he said. His voice came out as a croak. He made himself say it louder. "Luke, can you hear me? Luke?"

Nothing moved. Even the air was totally still. All he could hear was his own breathing.

How long did the spell take to work?

Darren picked the doll up again. Maybe he had to hold onto it. He hugged it close to his chest. "Luke? Come on! Luke! I'm here. Can you hear me? Luke?"

His eyes had started to burn. He rubbed them hard with his sleeve. He wasn't going to cry. He wouldn't cry, because this was going to work. It *had* to work.

"Luke!" he shouted. "I'm here. I'm here! Talk to me. Luke! Where are you? *Luke!*" By now he was close to screaming.

There was no one to hear. He waited by the grave for over an hour.

But Luke's ghost never came.

******

Darren sat by the grave and cried until he felt sick. They weren't sad tears. He was too angry to be upset.

It wasn't fair! He'd done it all right. He'd dug up dirt from his friend's grave! It should have worked.

But it hadn't. Mad Mary's so-called spell was a load of crap.

"Stupid old bitch," he said. He wiped his eyes.

She'd made it all up. That was her idea of fun. Trying to trick him into going out to dig up her grave. And he'd fallen for it. He'd tried to use her fake spell when it really mattered.

She'd laugh her head off if she could see him now.

But she'd never know, because she was dead.

And dead people didn't come back.

Darren gave the useless doll a kick. It didn't go very far. He ran after it and kicked it again. This time it flew all the way down the hill. He heard it land down at the bottom.

He nearly left it down there. But what if it had fallen on a grave? Someone might come to visit and see it.

He shone the torch down the hill. It took a moment to find the doll. It was all the way over by the side wall. He made his way down to it.

There was a grave there. But it didn't look like anyone came to visit it. The small, flat stone had thick moss all over it. Darren had to stand right up close to make out the words.

It read –

Mary Maxwell

1897–2003

Darren gasped and took a step back.

It was Mad Mary's grave.

Chapter 6
Dreams and Shadows

Darren's heart raced. Of all the places the doll could have landed ... He hadn't even known Mad Mary's grave was here.

For a moment he was sure she knew what he'd done. He'd used the spell on Luke, not her. He'd called her a bitch. Now she'd rise from the grave to make him pay.

But nothing happened. After a minute or so, his heart began to slow down. He took a few deep breaths.

He was being stupid. It was just chance that the doll had landed here. Of course Mad Mary was buried near Luke. She'd lived in the same area. She hadn't died that long ago. It would be odd if her grave *wasn't* around here.

She'd never had real magic. The grave doll had proved that. It had been a lie all along.

"Bitch," Darren said again, and spat on the stone.

He threw the doll over the graveyard wall into some trees and went home.

****

It was midnight by the time Darren got in. His mum tried ask him if it was OK, but he just walked past her. He was in no mood to talk to anyone right now.

He stomped into the bathroom and slammed the door. His eyes were still red and sticky from all the crying. He scrubbed his face until the skin was sore.

Darren stared at his face in the mirror. He looked pale and sick. There were big black bags under both his eyes. It looked like he'd been punched in the face.

He wasn't angry any more. He was just tired. So tired he could die. He felt like he was a hundred years old.

As old as Mad Mary had been. How was that fair? She'd been a mad, evil old lady. Yet she'd got to live to over a hundred. Luke hadn't even made it to 16.

How was that fair?

He switched off the light. As he turned to go, he looked back at the mirror. It took a second for what he saw to sink in.

He wasn't alone in the room.

Darren's heart stopped. He spun to look behind him.

There was no one there. He looked at the mirror again. This time all he saw was his own face. He took a slow, wobbly breath.

It must have been a shadow. The curtains moving in the wind. He was still a bit freaked out from earlier. That was why he'd thought it was a face.

That was why he'd thought he'd seen Mad Mary.

****

Darren went to bed. He felt worn out, but he couldn't sleep. His brain was in too much of a mess.

He kept thinking about Luke. Stupid stuff, like how he used to wear odd socks on exam days. The way he used to hum when Darren was trying to think. How he would fold his pizza in half before he ate it.

Things Luke did that no one else did. Things that were all gone now. Because Luke was all gone now.

And there was no magic spell to bring him back.

It took Darren hours to fall asleep. When he did, he had dark, nasty dreams.

He dreamed that he was walking home from school. He could see Luke up ahead, but Luke hadn't seen him.

Darren ran and ran, but he couldn't catch up. He shouted, but Luke didn't look back. He just kept on walking.

In the dream it switched to night-time. They came to the gates of the graveyard. Luke went in, and Darren ran after him.

The graves were all lit up by candles. Every one of them had the same name on it. Luke's name. But the words weren't carved into the stone.

They were written in blood.

Then he saw Luke on top of the hill. His back was turned, but Darren could see his blond hair. He'd stopped moving at last.

"Luke!" Darren shouted. He ran up the hill. There was no grass on it now. It was just a big mound of black dirt.

Luke was standing in front of a coffin. The same one that he'd been buried in. It was open, and Darren could see it was full of blood.

But he didn't care about that.

"Luke!" he said again. He put his hand on Luke's shoulder. "Didn't you hear me shouting? I was right behind you. Luke?" He pulled at Luke's arm to get his attention.

But the face that turned to look at him wasn't Luke's. It was the grinning skull of the grave doll.

Its teeth were sharp as needles. Darren could see they were red with fresh blood. *"Blood is life,"* it said in a rasping voice. *"Blood is life. Blood is life ..."*

The doll reached out for him with its claws. Darren stepped back, but there was no ground under his feet. He sank right through the dirt and fell into darkness. He fell, and fell, and fell ...

And woke up in his bed.

Chapter 7
Dead Things

Darren left the house the next day in a rotten mood. The last thing he wanted to do was go to school. But where else was he going to go? There was no point bunking off. It was no fun without Luke.

As he got out on the street, he was hit by a bad smell. He had to cover his mouth and nose with his hand. It was like something had died out here.

It turned out that something had. There was a bunch of dead birds on Mad Mary's front lawn. Two magpies, a crow, and what might have been a sparrow. It was hard to tell, because it didn't have a head.

Darren gagged.

The birds must have been left there by a cat. But they hadn't been killed for food. They'd been killed just for fun. The idea made him feel sick. He walked on quickly.

At the end of the street, Darren saw a dead rat. On the next road were two more dead birds. It was like there was death all around him.

Was it always like this? Maybe he just hadn't noticed until now. Maybe he just hadn't looked for it.

Birds died all the time. Rats died. *People* died. It didn't matter how old they were. It didn't matter if it was fair. They just died.

Darren got to school just as the bell rang. There was a buzz of noise in the corridors. He picked up a few words as he passed.

"Did you see that dead fox?" one boy was saying. "It didn't have any *eyes*."

"I saw, like, ten dead birds," another kid said.

"My aunt's dog was killed last night," he heard a girl say. "She was so upset …"

There were lots of stories going round. A tiger had got loose from the zoo. It was the work of a mad pet-killer. It was some kind of killer disease.

Darren couldn't stand it. He wanted to scream and shout at them all. What did it matter? It was just a load of animals. What about *Luke?* He was dead too! Why was no one talking about him?

It was like it was old news. Like no one but Darren even cared.

43

It only got worse when he got to his own class. Lisa Smith was in floods of tears.

"I came out and I found him there in his hutch – dead!" she sobbed. "He was only a baby. Who could do that? Poor little Snowy! We only had him for a few months."

Then why are you so upset? Darren thought. It was nasty, but he didn't care. He hadn't burst into tears like that when Luke had died. He'd been too numb to do anything. So how could she make such a fuss about a pet?

And yet all the girls were crowding round to hug her. Some of the others were even crying too.

"What is wrong with you?" Darren didn't know he was going to yell until it came out. "It's a bloody rabbit! They live, like, five years anyway! It's not like it's – It's not as if you ..."

He couldn't even get the words out. His legs were shaking. He felt like he was going to be sick.

The whole class was staring at him. He tried to speak again, but what came out was more like a sob. He turned and ran out of the room.

Darren could feel tears running down his face. He rubbed his eyes hard with his sleeve. Why was he crying? He wasn't upset, he was angry.

It was much easier to be angry. He wanted to shout and swear and smash things. He didn't want to cry. He didn't want to keep thinking about Luke, dead, in the ground …

He slammed into the boys' toilets. The bell had gone, so no one else was there. He glared at his face in the dirty mirror. He looked ill, and his eyes were red.

Darren spun the cold tap. The sink was clogged up, but he didn't care. So what if he flooded the floor? It didn't matter. None of this crap mattered.

He splashed cold water on his face. It didn't help him feel much better. He was dizzy and his skin felt too hot. He stood with his head down, breathing hard.

What was he meant to do now? Go back to class? What was the point? It was all so stupid.

Luke was *dead*. How could Darren just go on with life? How could he go to lessons and act like things were normal? It was crazy.

And yet it seemed like everyone else could do it. What was wrong with them?

What was wrong with *him*?

He looked up at the mirror.

Mad Mary was standing right behind him.

Chapter 8
Drowning

Darren froze. He saw Mad Mary smile in the mirror. She didn't have many teeth. The ones that were left were black or brown. Her teeth had looked like that when she was alive.

But they hadn't been half so sharp.

She looked dead. Her skin was the colour of candle wax. Her hair was like dry straw. Her eyes were sunk deep into her head.

In them, he saw nothing but hate.

"Thief!" she snarled. Her voice was deep and rasping. It was like the doll's voice in his dream. "Traitor! So many years. So many years in the ground ..."

Darren tried to turn, but she was too fast for him. Her bony hands closed around his neck. They were as cold and dead as frozen meat. She forced him down towards the sink.

He had no chance to fight. The ghost was just too strong. His chest hit the edge of the sink and he lost his breath. Before he could gasp in more, his face was in the water.

He choked. Water flooded his mouth and nose. It filled his eyes. He couldn't see anything but white.

He couldn't breathe.

This couldn't be happening. But Darren knew it was no dream. Dreams didn't make your nose burn and your chest hurt.

He was drowning. And there was nothing he could do to stop it.

He grabbed the sides of the sink, and tried to push himself up. But Mad Mary was as strong as steel. It was like trying to lift a car. He couldn't make her let him go.

The white of the sink was turning grey. He could see coloured lights. His chest felt like it was being crushed. Darren knew he was about to pass out. If he did, he would drown for sure.

He just had time to think: *Well, at least I'll be with Luke –*

– And then suddenly he was free.

His head burst out of the water like a cannon ball. He gasped in air. It hurt. It was as if his lungs had been burned. Water ran out of his eyes and down his face.

The room slowly came back into focus. Darren saw his pale face in the mirror.

But he didn't see Mad Mary.

He looked around. The floor was soaked and so was he, but he was alone. It was as if the ghost had never even been there. He stood still for a moment, panting.

Why had she left?

The door behind him flew open. Darren spun to face it, ready to fight. But it wasn't the ghost. It was Josh, one of the boys from his class.

"Hey. You all right, mate?" Josh asked. He looked a bit shocked.

Darren could guess what a mess he looked. He could feel the water dripping down his back.

"Yeah," he said. "I'm OK."

Josh didn't look like he believed it. "So are you coming to Art, then?" he asked. "The bell's gone."

"Maybe." Darren gave a shrug. "What do you care?"

"Just *asking*." Josh held up his hands. "Fine! I'll go." He backed out of the room.

Darren let out a sigh of relief.

His heart was just beginning to slow down. His chest still hurt. His neck was sore where the ghost's claws had dug into it.

It had been real. Mad Mary had just tried to kill him.

And that meant he'd been wrong last night. The grave doll had worked. It just hadn't worked on Luke.

Darren felt dizzy all of a sudden. He sat down hard on the wet floor.

What had he done?

All he'd wanted was a chance to see Luke again. He hadn't thought of it as trying to raise the dead. Luke should never have died in the first place. So how could it be wrong to try and bring him back? The spell would either

51

work or it wouldn't. He'd never dreamed that it could go this wrong.

Now Mad Mary's ghost was on the loose. It had to be her who'd killed all those animals. *Blood is life.* That was what she'd said. Killing things must make her stronger.

She'd tried to kill him. Darren hoped she wouldn't try again too soon. But he knew she *would* come after him.

And he couldn't be her only target. Mad Mary had hated a lot of people. Would she start to kill them off one by one?

He had to stop her. Maybe he was the only one who could. He was the only one who knew about the grave doll.

He had to find it and destroy it. Dump out the blood and dirt. Maybe that would send her ghost away again.

Darren had to hope that it would. Because if it didn't, he had no idea what to do.

Chapter 9

Back to the Graveyard

Darren didn't try to sneak out of school. He just walked out of the front gates. He didn't care if anyone saw him. What did school matter now?

It was a long way to the graveyard. He set off at a jog. It wasn't long before he was out of breath. His chest still hurt from earlier.

He was lucky to be alive. If Josh hadn't come along when he had ...

Darren knew it was luck that had saved him. He couldn't fight Mad Mary's ghost. If she came after him again, he was dead.

He just had to pray he could find the grave doll first.

The graveyard was still and silent when he got to it. That was good, but it was also a bit spooky. He felt like he was the only person for miles.

At least he didn't have to climb the walls this time. The front gates were open.

Darren's feet crunched on the grass as he walked in. At first he thought it was just dead leaves. Then he looked down.

It was insects. The ground was covered in them. They were all dead.

More of Mad Mary's work. It had to be.

Darren could see it in his mind. She'd risen from the dead, but she'd been weak at first. She'd needed more blood to get stronger. So she'd started small. At first she could only kill bugs. Then she'd moved on to birds. Then on to bigger things.

And then she'd come after him.

And what if she had killed him? How much power would his blood have given her?

Too much. He had to stop her, and not just to save his own life. If she killed him, she'd get even stronger. And no one else would know what to do.

Darren looked at the trees on the other side of the wall. He'd thrown the doll in there somewhere. But where? It had been dark, and he hadn't paid much attention. He could spend ages hunting for it.

He decided to go up the hill. Maybe he'd be able to see over the wall better from up there. He jogged back up towards Luke's grave.

It was bright and sunny up on top of the hill. All the same, Darren felt chilled. Maybe it was because of his wet shirt.

Or maybe it was something else. He went still as he noticed the smell.

Dirt, fresh flowers ... and blood.

In sort of a daze, he walked over to Luke's grave.

A dead crow lay on top of it. Its wings were spread out. On the grave marker he saw words painted in blood.

You're next.

Darren let out a snarl of rage. "You *bitch*," he said out loud. He picked the dead bird up by the wing and flung it away.

How dare she? She didn't need to do *this*. It was just a way to hurt Darren. He tore off his coat and used it to wipe the blood off the grave marker.

"I'll get her, Luke," he said to the grave. "Don't worry."

He stood up and looked out over the trees. Mad Mary's grave was down on the right just in front of the wall. So when he threw the doll, it must have landed ...

There! He could see a white shape up in one of the trees. The grave doll must be caught up in the branches. All he had to do was hop over the wall and shake it down.

"I win," Darren said with a cold smile. He ran down the slope towards the doll.

Too fast, as it turned out. He was nearly at the wall when his foot got caught. He tripped and fell flat on his face.

"Ow." Darren groaned and sat up. He looked to see what it was he'd tripped on.

It was a grave stone. He wasn't at all surprised to see the name on it.

Mad Mary's grave. He scowled down at it. Then he stopped and stared.

There were cracks all over the stone. Where had they come from? It hadn't been like that before. Surely he couldn't have done that just by kicking it.

Even as he watched, the cracks spread. It was like seeing glass break in slow motion.

Darren jumped up as fast as he could. He backed away from the stone.

He didn't get far. As he put his foot down, it sank right through the soil. The next thing he knew he was falling.

A pit had opened up in the earth. He fell a long way down and hit the bottom with a thud. He couldn't even yell. The fall knocked the air out of his lungs.

Dirt rained down on him from above. He coughed and brushed it off his face.

More came down after it. Darren looked up. The top of the hole seemed small and far away. Dirt was still pouring down into it.

It was already up to the tops of his shoes. If he didn't get out soon, he'd be buried alive.

Chapter 10
Buried Alive

A laugh floated down from above. It was like the rusty creak of an old door. Darren's skin went cold.

Mad Mary's ghost had returned.

He scrabbled at the sides of the pit. There was no way to get a grip on them. The dirt was just too loose. His fingers dug chunks out of the wall.

The hole was filling up fast. There was earth half-way up to his knees. He couldn't dig his way out of it. It was like quicksand. His feet just sank in deeper.

There was dirt in his hair and down the back of his neck. It filled his mouth and nose when he breathed. It got in his eyes. All Darren could see was a blur.

He couldn't get out of the pit. He was going to die down here.

"Help!" he shouted, and thumped at the sides of the pit. "Someone help me! Help!"

He knew it was no good. There was no one up there to hear.

And the dirt just kept pouring in.

Darren tried to jump. He didn't get anywhere near the top of the pit. It was a good metre out of his reach. As he landed, he just knocked more earth down on top of him.

"Help!" Darren yelled, his voice hoarse. He coughed up dirt. "Please. I'm down here! Help me!"

There was no answer. Not even from Mad Mary. She'd left him down here to die.

And he was going to. The dirt was nearly up to his arms now. He couldn't try to jump any more. He couldn't even shout. He was coughing too hard. It felt like he was going to cough up his lungs.

But he couldn't just give up and die. He stretched up one more time ...

... And someone took hold of his hand. Strong arms pulled him up out of the pit.

Darren fell out onto the grass. He lay on his belly and gasped for air.

He tried to look up at the person who'd saved him. He could see only a blurry shape. He had mud in his eyes. Everything was dark. Where had the sun gone?

Before he could say anything, he heard a terrible screech. It was like an air raid siren. A howl that went on and on and on.

Mad Mary knew that he'd escaped. And she wasn't happy.

The wind grew even stronger. It tore at his clothes and hair. Chunks of mud and rock rained down like missiles. This time the ghost was planning to batter him to death.

Well, she could do it. He wasn't strong enough to get up and run. Mad Mary had won. She had beaten him.

But that didn't mean anyone else had to die.

"Go!" Darren shouted to the person who'd pulled him out of the pit. "Get out of here!" He was the one that Mad Mary wanted dead. No one else needed to die.

But the person didn't go. Darren felt hands tugging at him, trying to pull him to his feet. He scrubbed at his eyes as he stood up. A rock as big as his fist hit his back.

"Get out of here!" he shouted again. He started to turn to look at the person who'd helped him. "I'm the one she's after! You've got to –"

His words were cut off as the person pushed him forward. He could see the wall in front of him now. And he could see the grave doll. It hung there in the trees, grinning down at him.

Darren began to run towards the wall.

The ghost's screaming got louder, more shrill. Bits of tree struck the ground all round him. A rock just missed his head and flew on to hit the wall. It left a dent as big as a plate.

Darren kept on running. He was headed at the wall far too fast. But if he slowed down Mad Mary would smash him to bits with rocks.

Darren put on a burst of speed and jumped at the wall.

His fingers just grazed the top of it. It took all his strength to hold on. The wind was trying to suck him down.

If he fell, he wouldn't get another try. Even the bricks were wobbling in the wind. It felt like the whole wall was about to come down.

Darren kicked his legs, and tried to get higher. In his mind, he saw the dead crow left on Luke's grave. If he fell now, no one would know how to stop Mad Mary. No one would make her pay for the things she'd done.

Darren pulled himself up on top of the wall. The grave doll was right above his head. He stood up to reach for it.

As he did, he saw a tree stump flying towards him. It would smash into him in less than a second.

He had two choices. Jump back down to save his life ... or get the doll.

He grabbed for the doll.

Chapter 11
Shattered

Darren's hand took hold of the doll. At the same moment, the tree stump hit him in the stomach.

It was like being kicked by a horse. It knocked him right off the top of the wall. As he hit the ground, he heard the crack of a bone breaking.

He didn't feel any pain. He was too stunned to feel much at all. He was sure he was about to pass out. He could see glowing lights in the sky.

Then he saw that the lights weren't just in his head.

The dark clouds were peeling away. Rays of sun were starting to spill through. The wind had died down to a soft breeze.

And Mad Mary's screech was now just a whisper.

Darren looked up. He saw the shape of the ghost. She was coming towards him.

But with each step, the shape got more and more faint. By the time she stood over him, he could only just see her.

"Traitor," she croaked. "You will pay. You will pay ..."

She made a slash at him with her claw-like nails. But she was gone before it had a chance to hit.

Darren closed his eyes. He hurt all over. But it didn't feel like he'd broken a bone. So what had made that crack? He sat up and looked down at himself.

He still had the grave doll in his hand. But all he was holding was its body. The grinning skull had been smashed like an egg. It must have hit the ground even harder than he had.

He threw his head back and laughed like an idiot.

Darren stood up. His legs shook. The graveyard was a mess. It looked like a bomb had gone off. He felt bad about it, but there was no way he could clean it up. He was so worn out, he wanted to just lie down and die.

He should have died. He would have died, if someone hadn't saved him. He looked around to see where the person who'd pulled him out of the grave had gone. They couldn't have got far …

But there was no one else. The graveyard was still and quiet. So was the road outside.

He was totally alone.

****

Darren limped back to his house. He knew what a state he must look. He was covered in mud, scrapes and bruises. But he didn't care right now. Let people stare.

As it turned out, no one did. They had bigger things to stare at.

When Darren got back to his street, he saw blue flashing lights. There were fire engines and police cars. His heart went cold.

"What's happened?" he asked. He tried to push through the crowd. He was sure something had happened to his house.

But he was wrong. His house looked the same as ever – apart from one small thing. It no longer had a house next to it.

Where Mad Mary's house had been, there was just rubble.

"It was the weirdest thing," said one of the men from up the street. "It was like a whirlwind. Just came out of nowhere. And it only hit that one single house. It was just crazy." He shook his head.

Darren hid his smile. He knew what had happened. No one else ever would ... but he could live with that. It had all been his fault, after all.

He went and sat down on a wall across the road. He watched people poke around in the ruins.

He was sure that they wouldn't find anything. Mad Mary was gone for good this time. Darren had won.

But he hadn't done it on his own. He wished he knew who'd helped him in the graveyard. How had they known he needed help? And why had they left so quickly? Darren hadn't even had a chance to see them.

He looked over to the trees at the end of the road. Someone slim and blond stood in the shadows there. They held up a hand to give Darren a wave.

Darren froze. "Luke?" he said, with dry lips. He started to stand up.

As he did, one of the fire engines pulled out. It drove in front of him.

By the time he could see again, Luke was gone.

But Darren knew that he'd been there.

Barrington Stoke would like to thank all its readers for commenting on the manuscript before publication and in particular:

Selena Beswick
Becky Bevans
Charlotte Boosey
Sam Brown
Alfie Burr
Jack Fisher
Sarah Flynn
Megan Glendon
Gloria Goodsell
Ashley Kelly
James Marsh

Thomas Matheron
Rae Moulding
Stuart Noonan
Sam Owen
Jake Pocknell
Tom Read
Billie Reynolds
Sam Taylor
Amy Terry
Danielle Thompson
Jack Walsh

Become a Consultant!

Would you like to give us feedback on our titles before they are published? Contact us at the email address below – we'd love to hear from you!

info@barringtonstoke.co.uk
www.barringtonstoke.co.uk

Great reads – no problem!

Barrington Stoke books are:

Great stories – from thrillers to comedy to horror, and all by the best writers around!

No hassle – fast reads with no boring bits, and a story that doesn't let go of you till the last page.

Short – the perfect size for a fast, fun read.

We use our own font and paper to make it easier to read our books. And we ask teenagers like you, who want a no-hassle read, to check every book before it's published.

That way, we know for sure that every Barrington Stoke book is a great read for everyone.

Check out www.barringtonstoke.co.uk for more info about Barrington Stoke and our books!